CW00890481

Scholastic Children's Books,
Commonwealth House, 1-19 New Oxford Street,
London WC1A 1NU, UK
a division of Scholastic Ltd

London ~ New York ~ Toronto ~ Sydney ~ Auckland

First published in the UK by Hippo, an imprint of Scholastic Ltd, 1998

Text Copyright © Abbey Communications Ltd, 1998
© Copyright in original stories and characters Enid Blyton Limited
Enid Blyton ™ Enid Blyton's signature is a trademark of Enid Blyton Limited
Audio-visual series © Copyright Abbey Home Entertainment Limited, 1998
Script adaptation by Caryn Jenner
Story consultant – Gillian Baverstock

ISBN 0 590 11180 9

Printed in Hong Kong

10 9 8 7 6 5 4 3 2 1

Enid Blyton's™
ENCHANTED LANDS

The Land of
Know-Alls

Joe, Beth and Fran ran through the Enchanted Wood. But as the children approached the Faraway Tree, they stopped and looked at it in horror. The leaves were brown and shrivelled.

"Oh no!" cried Fran. "What's happened?"

Moonface and Silky the fairy met the children.

"What's wrong with the tree?" Joe asked them.

"The Faraway Tree is dying," said Moonface sadly.

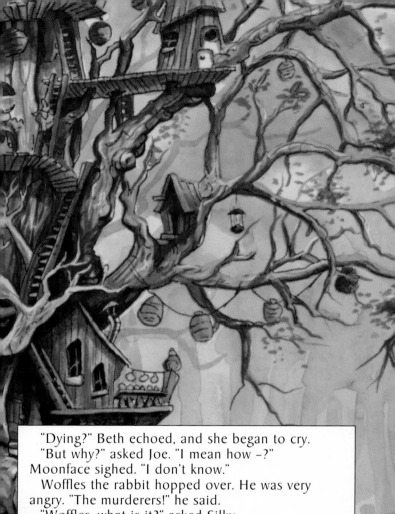

"Dying?" Beth echoed, and she began to cry.

"But why?" asked Joe. "I mean how –?"

Moonface sighed. "I don't know."

Woffles the rabbit hopped over. He was very angry. "The murderers!" he said.

"Woffles, what is it?" asked Silky.

"A bunch of trolls are under the tree digging for jewels." Woffles answered.

7

Moonface and Joe followed Woffles down into his burrow. At the bottom of the burrow was a tunnel, and at the end of the tunnel was a door with a window in it. The door was locked, but through the window, they could see the trolls digging for gems. They were chopping through the roots of the Faraway Tree.

"Look, Timmy," one of the trolls said. He picked up a sparkling stone. "'Ere's a big one!"

"Lovely, Robin!" said Timmy.

The two trolls lifted their pickaxes, ready to dig out the stone from the tree roots.

"STOP THAT!" shouted Moonface. "STOP THAT AT ONCE! You're killing the tree!"

Suddenly, the biggest troll appeared in the window.
"So?" he said. "It's only a tree."
"It's the Faraway Tree," Joe told him.
The troll sniggered. "Well, sonny, unless the rest of you wants to be far away from your head, I suggest you push off and let us get on with our work."

Moonface tried to open the door, but it didn't budge. "Is there another way in?" he asked Woffles.

"Not that I know of," Woffles answered.

Joe sighed. How were they going to save the Faraway Tree from the trolls?

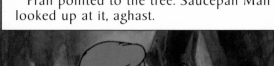

Fran, Beth and Silky were waiting anxiously near Woffles' burrow when they heard a clanking sound. It was Saucepan Man.

"Why the long faces?" he asked.

"It's the tree," said Fran glumly.

"A bee?" said Saucepan Man. His pots and pans made so much noise that he didn't hear very well. "Did you get stung by a bee?"

Fran pointed to the tree. Saucepan Man looked up at it, aghast.

Just then, Woffles, Moonface and Joe arrived.

"The trolls have locked themselves in beneath the tree," said Moonface. "They're tearing the roots out and –"

"The Land of Know-Alls!" said Saucepan Man.

"Of course!" Moonface cried. "It's just arrived at the top of the tree!"

"The Know-Alls know everything," said Silky. "If anyone can help us save the tree, they can."

The children and their friends climbed the tree and went up into the hole to the Land of Know-Alls. A glittering palace stood in front of them.

"Come on," said Moonface, "We must hurry."

The enormous doors opened automatically and the group passed to the Great Hall. Light shone through the crystal walls and roof. The palace was magnificent!

14

A Know-All sat at a desk near the door.

"Look at the size of his head!" Joe whispered.

The Know-All smiled. "It has to be big to hold everything I know."

"I'm sorry. I didn't mean –"

"No offence taken," said the Know-All. "Mind you, if you think my head is big, wait until you meet the Great Know-All."

"That's who we've come to see," said Moonface.

"The Faraway Tree," the Know-All interrupted. "And the trolls. I know. This way, please."

The Know-All led them to a crystal lift in the centre of the hall. He pointed upwards and the lift floated up and into another room.

The Great Know-All stood
waiting for them.
  "Your most gracious
Knowledgability,"
Moonface
greeted him.
"Many thanks for
this audience."
  "There is no need for
this formality,
Moonface," said the
Great Know-All.
"Welcome everyone, to
the Land of Know-Alls."
  The children and their
Faraway friends gathered
round to hear the Great
Know-All speak. They
listened to his wise
words, thanked him,
then hurried back
down the ladder to the
Enchanted Wood. They
were determined to
save the Faraway Tree,
but there was no
time to lose!

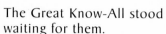

On the ground, Woffles heard shrieks of excitement. He hopped out of the way just as the children and their friends slid on to the soft grass beneath the Faraway Tree.

At once the friends spread out and started to look closely at the grassy mounds near the tree. Woffles watched curiously.

"What are you looking for?" he asked.

"The Great Know-All told us about a secret entrance," explained Fran.

Suddenly, Beth gave a shout.

"It's here!"

Everyone gathered round as she opened the trap door.

"Well, well," said Woffles. "Lived here all my life, I have, and I never knew about that!"

"Well, you aren't a Know-All," said Joe.

"Come on!" said Beth. "We've got a tree to save."

The secret door led to the roots of the Faraway Tree.

"Look, Timmy!" said Robin. "It's that big-headed tree-lover again!"

"He's brought his little friends with him," said Timmy.

Moonface confronted the trolls. "We want you to leave at once," said Moonface.

"Yeah?" said the biggest troll. "What if we don't? What are you going to do about it?"

"Ha, ha, ha!" the three trolls laughed.

"We'll set this on you," threatened Fran and held out her hand. The trolls looked at the little green caterpillar in Fran's hand.

"Hee, hee, hee!" the trolls laughed harder.

"Have you heard of the Great Know-All?" Silky asked them. "He gave us this caterpillar."

The trolls laughed and laughed. Silky touched the caterpillar with her wand.

The caterpillar grew and grew and grew! It had big teeth and it didn't look very pleased. The trolls stopped laughing. They stared at the giant caterpillar in horror.

"Eustace? Timmy?" Robin asked the other trolls. "Is that what I think it is?"

The caterpillar opened its mouth.

"ROOOAAAAARRR!!"

"Yes!" shouted Eustace and Timmy.

"In that case –"

"We'd better –"

"Run!!!"

22

The trolls ran as fast
as they could and
the giant caterpillar
chased them into the
depths of the earth.

The children and their friends climbed back through the secret door.

"I don't think the trolls will be back in a hurry!" laughed Joe.

"We might have got rid of the trolls, but the Faraway Tree doesn't look any better," sighed Beth, "I hope it's not too late."

"We still have one more gift from the Great Know-All," Silky reminded her.

Beth looked at the small box that Moonface took out of his pocket. "It's hard to think that there's enough magic in that little tin to make the tree better," she said.

"Well, here goes," said Moonface,
as he opened the lid of the box.
The children held their breaths.

The magic whizzed out of the
box, in all the colours of the
rainbow. The tree dwellers
peeped through their windows.
   Everyone watched in wonder as
the magic swirled round the tree.

The tree trunk suddenly looked straighter, and the branches seemed stronger. Green leaves sprouted and flowers blossomed.

The children laughed with joy and tried to catch the magic sparkles that twinkled and fell to the ground.

"Hooray!" shouted Joe and Beth, dancing round the tree.

Fran looked up towards the top of the Faraway Tree.

"Thank you," she whispered. "Thank you so much."

"Who are you talking to?" Beth asked her.

"He knows," she said, with a secret smile. "He knows all."